Frog

Huggums

Bun Bun

Little Sister

Gator

Bat Child

Maurice & Molly

Oscar

A GREEN FROG PUBLISHERS, INC./J. R. SANSEVERE BOOK

LITTLE SISTER'S BRACELET

BY MERCER MAYER

RANDOM HOUSE 🏠 NEW YORK

Little Sister put on her new bracelet. She took her pail and went to play with her friends.

But she lost her bracelet
while she was playing.

"I lost my new bracelet,"
cried Little Sister.
"We will find it for you," said Max.

"Don't worry,"
said Skat Owl.

"I can look from the treetops," said Max.

"I can look from the hilltops," said Mooso.

"I can look from
high in the sky,"
said Skat Owl.

Possum Child said,
"I can look
under things."

Mouse said,
"I can look inside things."

Bat Child said,
"I can search
in dark places."

Malcom sniffed around on the ground.

Bun Bun looked under the briar bushes.

Mooso looked behind
the tree.

Little Critter fished for it.

Frog and Gator swam for it.

Maurice and Molly dug for it.

They all searched high and low, but
no one could find Little Sister's bracelet.

There was just one place
where no one thought to look.